DARK HUNTER

THE MARSH DEMON

First published 2013 by
A & C Black, an imprint of Bloomsbury Publishing Plc
50 Bedford Square, London, WC1B 3DP

www.bloomsbury.com

Copyright © 2013 A & C Black
Text copyright © 2013 Benjamin Hulme-Cross
Illustrations copyright © 2013 Nelson Evergreen

The right of Benjamin Hulme-Cross and Nelson Evergreen to be
identified as the author and illustrator of this work has been asserted
by them in accordance with
the Copyrights, Designs and Patents Act 1988.

ISBN 978-1-4081-8070-9

A CIP catalogue for this book is available from the British Library.

Printed and bound by CPI Group (UK) Ltd, Croydon CR0 4YY

1 3 5 7 9 10 8 6 4 2

Catch Up is a not-for-profit charity
which aims to address the problem of
underachievement that has its roots in
literacy and numeracy difficulties.

DARK HUNTER

THE MARSH DEMON

BENJAMIN HULME-CROSS

ILLUSTRATED BY NELSON EVERGREEN

A & C BLACK
AN IMPRINT OF BLOOMSBURY
LONDON NEW DELHI NEW YORK SYDNEY

The Dark Hunter

Mr Daniel Blood is the Dark Hunter.
People call him to fight evil demons,
vampires and ghosts.

Edgar and Mary help Mr Blood with
his work.

The three hunters need to be strong and
clever to survive...

Contents

Chapter 1

Welcome

Mr Blood, Edgar and Mary arrived at the small town of Grimstock at noon.

The sun was high in the sky but the town looked dark and gloomy. But the people of the town were happy. They stood along the High Street waving and cheering as Mr Blood walked towards the town hall.

Mary smiled and waved back. Edgar
did not.

"People are always happy to see us arrive," Edgar said. "But it never seems to last."

Mary didn't listen to him. "Oh, I could get used to this!" she said.

"Keep alert," snapped Mr Blood. "You never know what is about to happen. We need to find out why they called us here."

They walked up some steps to the Town
Hall and went in.

Inside, the hall was packed with people. They were cheering and waving too.

Around the edges of the hall were tables laden with cakes and drinks. It looked like a huge fair.

Mr Blood led the way towards a large desk at the far end of the hall.

Behind the desk, a large, round man in a red gown stood up to greet them.

"I'm pleased to meet you, Mr Blood. Come and sit down."

He leaned over the desk to shake Mr Blood's hand and pointed to three chairs.

"Welcome to Grimstock," he said. "I am the Mayor."

"Ah," said Mr Blood. "It was you who sent for me. How may we help?"

"Plenty of time for that," said the Mayor. "You must be thirsty."

He nodded to someone in the crowd who placed a tray of drinks and cakes on the desk.

"You are kind," said Mr Blood. "But please tell us, why are we here?"

And so the Mayor told the story...

Chapter 2

The Storm

"Five years ago," the Mayor began, "a terrible storm blew across Grimstock on the darkest day of the year – Midwinter."

"It's Midwinter today," Edgar hissed to Mary.

"The storm lasted only a few hours, but in that time the town was damaged very badly," said the Mayor. "Trees fell across roads. Roofs were blown off buildings. Some houses were struck by lightning and caught fire. Ten people died."

The Mayor went on, "The worst of the
storm hit Wormley Marsh, just outside
the town. It was struck by huge bolts of
lightning over and over again. That storm
is the only thing that could have brought
the evil to this town."

"And what evil is that?" asked
Mr Blood.

"Well," the Mayor said, "at first we
knew nothing of it. In the year after the
storm, we rebuilt the town.

"The next Midwinter night, many of
us came here to the hall. We planned to
stay awake through the night. We wanted
to think about the people who died in the
storm."

The Mayor went on. "Outside, the night was quiet. But on the stroke of midnight, something in the air changed. A terrible smell blew through the town from the marsh. A few minutes later we heard screaming."

The Mayor stopped and wiped his brow.

"We all rushed outside to see what had happened. Two children were being carried off by... something. It was… It was a horror from hell."

"You will need to be more exact than that," said Mr Blood.

"Yes, of course," said the Mayor.
"The thing that carried the children was
some sort of giant. It had arms and legs.
It walked like a man. But it was as tall as
a house."

"It stank of the marsh," said the Mayor. "Its body seemed to be made of mud. We call it the marsh demon. The children were never seen again."

"And you think this marsh demon will come again?" asked Mr Blood.

"Yes sir. It is Midwinter," said the mayor. "It takes two children at midnight on Midwinter every year. But this year, our children will not die. You will kill the monster, Mr Blood. And if you do not, it will take your helpers, not our children."

The mayor looked over Mr Blood's shoulder and nodded.

A group of men jumped forward.

Two men pulled Edgar and Mary from their chairs and dragged them away.

Mr Blood shouted, "No!"

But there was nothing he could do to stop them.

Chapter 3

Prison

Mary and Edgar spent the rest of the day in a cell in the town prison.

They tried to stay calm, but after several hours Mary began to get angry. She shouted through the bars of their cell. She called the guards monsters, cowards and child-killers.

But the guards did not reply. Some of them even laughed at her.

"It's no good," said Edgar. "They don't want to lose more of their children. If anyone gets taken by the marsh demon, they want it to be us."

"Well, it won't happen," said Mary. "Mr Blood will have a plan. He always does."

"Let's hope so," said Edgar.
"But where is he?"

Outside, a bell rang eleven times.
It was one hour to midnight.

Heavy feet thumped towards the cell.
A group of guards opened the cell and
walked in. Mary spat at one of the men.

"I'm sorry, miss," he said. "But if we
don't do this, two of our children will die.
It's you or them."

The guards tied their hands behind their backs and walked them out into the night.

As they marched through the town, the streets were empty. No lights shone in windows. Nobody wanted the marsh demon to notice them.

Mr Blood was waiting for the children at the town hall.

"If you have hurt them," Mr Blood snarled at the guards, "I will find a way to set the demon on you."

"We're not hurt," said Mary. "Just get us away from these horrible men."

"Where is the Mayor?" asked Edgar.

"He didn't want to face the demon," said Mr Blood. "I suppose he is hiding under his bed, the fat toad."

"Come on!" barked a guard. "Not much time left."

They marched on to the edge of the town and a short way further. The stink of the marsh grew stronger.

The guards stopped.

"This is it," said a guard. "We will tie the children to the tree. If you cannot kill the marsh demon, it will take the first two children it can find."

"This is murder," said Mr Blood. "We came here to help you. You do not need to put my helpers in danger."

"We have our orders, sir," the guard replied.

The guards tied Edgar and Mary to a
large tree on the edge of the marsh and got
ready to leave.

Edgar and Mary looked at the marsh with fear. It was covered in thick mist.

"One more thing, sir," said the guard. "Do not try to untie the children. Several of my men will be watching from the town. They have bows and arrows. They are very good shots."

He looked hard at Mr Blood. "If you untie the children, we will pin them to the tree with arrows."

Mr Blood glared at the men.

"If you want this demon killed," he growled, "place your torches on the ground around the edges of the marsh."

The guards did as they were asked.
Then, one by one, they crept away.

Chapter 4

Midnight

It was midnight. In the distance, a single bell rang twelve times.

Edgar and Mary trembled. The tree creaked. Very slowly, the mist hanging over the marsh began to swirl. The marsh smell grew stronger.

Mr Blood stared hard into the dark. The torch flames flickered in the mist.

The marsh itself was hidden. It was a black, silent, stinking terror.

"The guards are gone," said Edgar. "Quick, untie us!"

"I'll try." Mr Blood's voice sounded strained.

He walked around the marsh towards Edgar and Mary.

"What are you doing?" asked Mary. "If you try to untie us, the men with bows will kill us."

"You'd rather wait and see what comes to get us?" Edgar spat.

Mary didn't reply.

Mr Blood was only a few steps away from Edgar and Mary when an arrow hissed through the air and thumped into the ground next to Edgar's foot.

Edgar yelped.

Mr Blood jumped back.

"So they meant it," said Mary. "Our only way to escape is to do what they want."

"Mr Blood..." said Edgar in a very quiet voice.

The mist had lifted. The black surface of the marsh moved slowly. The rotten mud was bubbling and steaming up through the ground.

It was forming a heap.

"It's coming," said Mr Blood. "We will fight the monster with fire."

"Does that work with marsh demons?" asked Mary.

Mr Blood didn't reply.

"You've never even seen one before, have you?" said Edgar. "*Look!*"

He pointed again at the marsh.

A huge mound of stinking mud was piling up a short way from the tree.

"Marshes burn," said Mr Blood. "So this monster will burn."

He picked up two of the torches.

"I am putting two torches behind the tree," said Mr Blood. "If I can untie you, take one each as a weapon."

"Is that the best plan you can think of?" Edgar yelled. "Wave a burning stick at it? We are all going to..."

The others never heard what Edgar was trying to say. An awful sound boomed across the marsh. It was a slow, hollow roar that seemed to go on for ever.

The mound of mud
began to unfold itself.

Chapter 5

Mud Monster

The marsh demon rose from the slime and stood above its victims.

It was huge. Rotten leaves and sticks stuck to its skin. It shook itself like a wet dog. Live eels and frogs fell from its mouth and sank back into the marsh.

In two huge steps the monster reached the edge of the marsh and looked down at Edgar and Mary.

Mr Blood ran forward and pushed a flaming torch into the monster's belly.

The flames fizzled out. The monster roared again. With a swipe of one arm, it knocked Mr Blood out of the way.

Edgar shouted in terror.

The monster reached down and grabbed Mary's arm. She screamed and kicked, but the rope tying her to the tree held firm. She couldn't get free.

The monster snapped the rope.

Edgar and Mary both tried to reach the torches behind the tree. Mary got hold of one.

The monster pulled Edgar away before he could reach the other torch.

Then it grabbed Mary and held them both, one in each hand.

The marsh demon swung them high
up into the air until they were both staring
into the monster's foul face. It opened its
evil mouth.

"No!" screamed Edgar, closing his eyes.

He heard an even louder roar from the monster – and it let go of him. He fell through the air and landed in the marsh with a muddy splash.

When he opened his eyes he could see the monster thrashing around wildly, huge flames leaping across its skin. It was roaring in pain.

It began to stumble towards the town.

Mary and Mr Blood rushed to the edge
of the marsh and pulled Edgar out.

"What happened?" he croaked.

"Mr Blood was right," said Mary,
shaking. "Fire. I stuck my torch down
the monster's throat."

"Will it die?" asked Edgar.

"Yes, in the end," said Mr Blood. "But some marshes can burn for days."

They all looked towards the town. The monster was crashing from house to house. The air was full of smoke and screaming.

"Should we help them?" said Edgar.

"We came here to help them, and they tried to feed you to a demon," said Mr Blood. "I think it's time we left them alone now. Don't you?"